nothing like a

For Keith and William
S. S.

For Olivia—
there's nothing like a daughter.
B. K.

First edition 2011

Library of Congress Cataloging-in-Publication Data is available.

Library of Congress Catalog Card Number 2010040796

ISBN 978-0-7636-3617-3

CCP 16 15 14 13 12 11
10 9 8 7 6 5 4 3 2 1

Printed in Shenzhen, Guangdong, China

This book was typeset in Caecilia Heavy.
The illustrations were created digitally.

Candlewick Press
99 Dover Street
Somerville, Massachusetts 02144

visit us at www.candlewick.com

puffin

SUE SOLTIS

illustrated by BOB KOLAR

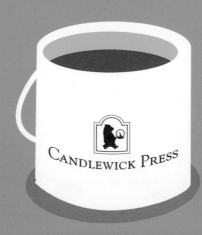

CANDLEWICK PRESS

Look, a puffin!
What a marvelous creature,
one of a kind and amazing.

Indeed, there is nothing like a puffin.

Take, for example, this ladder.
A ladder is nothing like a puffin.
It has steps you climb up
to get somewhere high.

A house is also nothing like a puffin.
A house has windows and doors.

Inside are sinks and chairs and beds.
A house is a place you can live in.

A newspaper, to be sure, is nothing like a puffin.
A newspaper is shaped like a rectangle
and made out of paper.

A newspaper has pages. It's black and white.

But wait—

a puffin is black and white, too!
What are the chances?

A newspaper is something
like a puffin, after all.

A pair of jeans, of course, is nothing like a puffin.
Jeans are blue.
Jeans have pockets and two legs.

Oh, no—don't say it.

Puffins have two legs, too!
Not another thing that's something
like a puffin. . . .

Look out for the goldfish!

Of course, a goldfish is
nothing like a puffin.
A goldfish has scales and fins.
A goldfish swims.

It looks like a puffin can swim, too.
A goldfish is a little bit,
a tiny little bit,
like a puffin.

So is a newspaper. So is a pair of jeans.
What could possibly be next?

Surely a shovel is nothing like a puffin.
A puffin isn't made out of wood and metal.
A puffin doesn't have a handle or a blade for digging.

Just a minute—a puffin uses its feet for digging.
A shovel is a little something like a puffin.
Who would have guessed?

Look here, a snake is nothing at all like a puffin.
A snake moves along without legs or wings.
Snakes hatch from eggs, just like birds.

Hold on a second. . . .

A puffin is a bird!
So it must have hatched from an egg, too.
A snake is something like a puffin.

That figures.

How about that helicopter?

A helicopter doesn't have two legs.
And it can't swim.
It's made out of metal and has a propeller.
A helicopter flies.

Watch out! This puffin can fly, too.
Even a helicopter is something like a puffin!

Maybe a puffin is not so amazing after all.
Maybe a puffin is not one of a kind.
Look at this penguin.

A penguin is black and white,
just like a puffin.
A penguin dives and swims.
So does a puffin.
A penguin is a bird.
So is a puffin.
A penguin has feathers,
and two wings,
and a beak,
and two feet!

There's no getting around it—
a penguin and a puffin are two of a kind.

But look—a penguin can't fly!

A penguin is more than a little like a puffin—
more than, say, a newspaper or a goldfish.
But it's not *exactly* like a puffin.

So it's true!
It's true, after all!

There's nothing like a puffin!